The BEST SEAT in Second Grade

story by Katharine Kenah

pictures by Abby Carter

SCHOLASTIC INC.

New York   Toronto   London   Auckland   Sydney
Mexico City   New Delhi   Hong Kong   Buenos Aires

To Nina, my first and forever best friend, with love
—K.K.

To Carter
—A.C.

ISBN-13: 978-0-545-01179-2
ISBN-10: 0-545-01179-5

12 11 10 9 8 7 6 5 4 3 2 1   7 8 9 10 11/0

Printed in the U.S.A.   23

This edition first printing, January 2007

Contents

Hamster Helper   5

Pocket Rider   15

The Animal Zone   29

Sam's Favorite Subject   37

Hamster Helper

Sam had the best seat

in second grade.

He sat at the back of Room 75.

He did not sit near the globe,

or the dinosaur models,

or the paper pioneer fort.

Sam sat beside

George Washington.

George Washington was small

and round and the color of honey,

and he sneezed.

George Washington was a hamster.

Sam loved George Washington

more than anything else at school.

George Washington was

Sam's favorite subject.

Sam's teacher, Mr. Hopper, asked,

"Who knows something about lava?"

"It pops out of volcanoes," said Sam,

"the way George Washington

pops out of his nest."

Someone in the front row giggled.

"Good answer!" said Mr. Hopper.

7

Every Monday Mr. Hopper
picked a new Hamster Helper.
The Hamster Helper got to feed
George Washington.

The Hamster Helper got to make
toys out of boxes and tubes.
The Hamster Helper got to play
with George Washington.

"Please, please, oh, please,"
Sam groaned. "Pick me!"
He crossed his fingers
and held his breath.

Mr. Hopper reached into

the bowl of names.

"Miguel!" he said.

"You are our new Hamster Helper."

"Oh, boy!" said Miguel.

"Oh, *no*," said Sam.

"It is never my turn."

Sam was tired of waiting

to be Hamster Helper.

He was sure George Washington

was tired of his cage.

Sam wanted to show

George Washington the world

outside of Room 75.

"Don't forget," Mr. Hopper reminded

his class. "Tomorrow is our trip

to the science museum.

Bring your coats,

bring your lunches,

and bring your permission slips."

Sam decided to bring

something *extra*.

Pocket Rider

The science museum was busy

and bright and crowded.

"Stay in your groups,"

called Mr. Hopper.

"The animal sticker on your name tag

will tell you which group you are in.

Grasshoppers stick together.

Frogs stick together.

Dolphins stick together.

We don't want anyone to get lost."

"Sam!" said Nina.

"Where is your name tag?"

"In my coat," Sam replied.

He reached deep into his pocket . . .

and patted George Washington.

Sam looked at the sticker

on his name tag. "I'm a Grasshopper."

"Good," said Nina. "I am, too."

The Grasshoppers and Frogs

and Dolphins hung up their coats.

"Sam," said Ollie. "It's warm in here.

Why don't you take off your coat?"

"I can't," Sam said quickly.

"I might catch a cold."

George Washington sneezed.

18

"Hurry up!" called Sophie.

"We are going to The Star Show

at the planetarium!"

Sam followed the other Grasshoppers.

He walked slowly and kept his hand

over his pocket.

The planetarium was round and dark.

The class wiggled and waited

in rows of seats.

When the first star twinkled above,

Sam took George Washington

out of his pocket.

"Make a wish," he whispered.

George Washington sneezed.

No one noticed George Washington.

When the Grasshoppers whirled
through the wind tunnel,
George Washington's whiskers
blew backward.

When the Grasshoppers made faces

in front of the funny mirrors,

George Washington looked like

a furry beach ball with huge eyes.

No one noticed George Washington.

The Grasshoppers climbed

through a Giant Seashell.

They peered into

Homes of the Future.

They poked and laughed at

Bubbles Are a Blast.

George Washington watched

and listened and sneezed.

Finally Ollie sat on a bench.

"I can't walk another step," he said.

"I'm hungry," said Nina.

"I'm thirsty," said Miguel.

"Me, too," grumbled Sophie.

Sam did not want to eat lunch.

George Washington might smell

something yummy

and pop right out of his pocket.

"I'll catch up with you later,"

Sam said, as he dashed

down the hall.

"But, Sam!" Nina called.

"Where are you going?

Grasshoppers are supposed

to stick together."

The Animal Zone

Sam ran upstairs and saw a sign

for the Animal Zone.

He took a deep breath and said,

"Wait until you see what is here."

Sam held up George Washington
in front of each display.
They looked at baby rabbits
and baby chicks.
George Washington sneezed.

"Don't look," Sam whispered
when they reached a tank
of boa constrictors.
George Washington *trembled*.

31

"Now," said Sam,

"here is the best place of all!"

The Hamster Habitat

was a jumble of tubes and tunnels.

There were hamster-sized

seesaws and ladders and slides.

Hamsters were *everywhere*.

They were all small.

They were all round.

They were all the color of honey.

"Look," Sam whispered

to George Washington. "Family!"

Footsteps clattered down the hall
as the rest of the Grasshoppers
rushed toward Sam.

"There you are, Sam!"

they shouted.

"Are you all right?"

"I'm fine," said Sam. "I was just

showing the hamsters to—"

He stopped talking.

George Washington was in his hands.

George Washington was right in front

of Ollie, Miguel, Sophie, and Nina.

Everyone noticed George Washington.

"Sam!" cried Nina.

"What have you done?"

Before he could answer,

George Washington jumped

out of Sam's hands—

and into the Hamster Habitat!

Sam's Favorite Subject

Sam screamed. He did not move.

"Oh, no!" Sophie groaned.

Ollie yelled at Sam.

Nina yelled at Ollie.

Miguel shouted, "Help!"

Mr. Hopper hurried up the stairs

to the Animal Zone.

The Frogs and Dolphins

followed right behind him.

"What's wrong?" called Mr. Hopper.

The Grasshoppers pointed to Sam.

He pointed to the Hamster Habitat.

Sam moaned. "He's gone!"

"Who?" asked Mr. Hopper.

"George Washington," mumbled Sam.

"He's in there."

Everybody stared at the sea

of busy hamsters.

"There are too many of them,"

said the Frogs.

"We'll never find him,"

said the Dolphins.

"We have to *try*!"

said the Grasshoppers.

Sam's whole class

spread out around the sides

of the Hamster Habitat.

"Look for something small,"

said Ollie.

"And round," said Miguel.

"And the color of honey," said Sophie.

They looked and looked

at hamsters climbing and digging,

at hamsters spinning and grooming,

at hamsters drinking and eating

and sleeping.

Sam stood still and watched one nest

shake and tremble like a volcano.

Suddenly a hamster popped

out of the nest . . .

just like lava.

The hamster was small

and round and the color of honey,

and it *sneezed*.

"George Washington!" cried Sam.

He reached down and scooped

their hamster into his hands.

Nina said, "I knew we'd find him.

George Washington is

Sam's favorite subject."

The next day, Sam carried

George Washington's cage

to the front of Room 75.

"I think he might be safer near you,"

he said.

Mr. Hopper smiled. "Good idea."

Sam walked slowly back to his seat.

"Class?" asked Mr. Hopper.

"Can you think of anything else

we should move up front?"

"Sam!" yelled the Frogs and Dolphins

and all of the Grasshoppers.

"Good answer," said Mr. Hopper.

George Washington sneezed.

Sam grinned and pushed his desk

to the front of Room 75.

For the rest of the year,

he sat between his teacher

and George Washington.

Sam had the best seat

in second grade.